T0154881

PRAGUE

Maude Veilleux

PRAGUE

Translated from the French by
Aleshia Jensen and Aimee Wall

QC FICTION

Revision: Peter McCambridge
Proofreading: David Warriner, Elizabeth West, Anna Prawdzik
Book design: Folio infographie
Cover & logo: Maison 1608 by Solisco
Fiction editor: Peter McCambridge

Copyright © Hamac. Publié avec l'autorisation de Hamac.
Originally published under the title *Prague*
Translation copyright © Aleshia Jensen and Aimee Wall

ISBN 978-1-77186-178-6 pbk; 978-1-77186-179-3 epub;
978-1-77186-180-9 pdf; 978-1-77186-181-6 mobi/pocket

Legal Deposit, 2nd quarter 2019
Bibliothèque et Archives nationales du Québec
Library and Archives Canada

Published by QC Fiction
6977, rue Lacroix
Montréal, Québec H4E 2V4
Telephone: 514 808-8504
QC@QCfiction.com
www.QCfiction.com

QC Fiction is an imprint of Baraka Books.

Printed and bound in Québec

Trade Distribution & Returns
Canada and the United States
Independent Publishers Group
1-800-888-4741
orders@ipgbook.com

We acknowledge the support from the Société de développement des entreprises culturelles (SODEC) and the Government of Québec tax credit for book publishing administered by SODEC.

Société
de développement
des entreprises
culturelles
Québec

Financé par le gouvernement du Canada
Funded by the Government of Canada | Canada

WE STARTED TALKING ABOUT PRAGUE as a joke. We were in a bar, already pretty drunk. I was reading *Vérité et amour* by Claire Legendre. He loved Kundera. I'd always dreamed of Prague without really knowing why. That's how the idea came up. We paid for our drinks, told the server we were leaving town the next week. We left and crossed the road to his apartment. We bought the tickets.

We didn't know each other well. We worked together at a bookstore. I was his boss.

We bought the tickets, then sat down on his bed. He put on some music. We talked. He tried to edge closer to me. I leaned back against the wall, hesitant, trying not to meet his gaze. I wanted him, but I had my period. I felt stupid for not cancelling. Another week had seemed too long to wait. I needed my dose of him. He found his way over to me. He leaned his forehead against the wall. Then we kissed. For a long time. He tried to slip his hands between my thighs. I ended up on my back. Him on top of me. I was wearing a black cotton dress, one I'd had forever. It used to be my mother's. I'd stolen it from her closet. There's a family photo with her wearing it, I must be around twelve, and she looks so pretty in it. The black had faded, but I still loved it. It was short, with cut-outs that showed off my sides. He pulled at the fabric and a seam split. I told him he could rip it. He slipped his hands into the holes at my sides and tore. The dress opened right down the front. I pulled what was left of it over my head and threw it to the floor while he unhooked my bra. He said: that's better.

I laughed. We looked at each other. His eyes were green like mine. Then he realized I had my period. I told him: I feel stupid. I should have stayed home.

He said: don't be silly.

I said: will you be mad if we don't have sex?

He said: no, I'm not the type to get mad about something like that.

We kissed again. I unbuckled his belt. He was hard. I started sucking his dick. He stroked my back, slid his hand down to my ass. He went to slip a finger inside.

He said: is that okay?

I said: yes, but it's distracting.

I stopped and moved up to kiss him. He put his finger in his mouth, then in mine, and then into my ass. Then a second finger. I turned to face away from him. I wanted more. He pretended to be afraid of hurting me. I guided him inside, my hand on his cock. I gently pushed back onto him. Then he took control. A few times, I put a hand on his hip. He slowed down. When I pinched him, he said: do you like that or does it hurt?

I said: both.

Neither of us came that night. He said: I have a hard time coming during sex.

I didn't respond. I didn't know what to say. Most of all I felt bad for him. I thought maybe it was me. Maybe I wasn't his type. I went to the bathroom. He got up too. He brought in two glasses of water. We fell asleep. That was the second time we had sex.

We both had to work in the morning. We didn't want to arrive together, didn't want to make it obvious. We decided that I would turn right and take the bus to the corner of Laurier and Parc. He'd go left and walk to the bookstore.

It worked. No one noticed.

: :

The first time we slept together, we had arranged to meet in a bar. We talked. A lot. He was anxious, full of guilt. He wanted to know more about the situation with my husband. Barely a year and a half into our marriage, we'd decided, each of us, to look elsewhere. We had no doubts about our love. Extramarital sex couldn't tarnish it. We were devoted to each other. I tried to explain. I wasn't looking for an out. I had no intention of interfering with his life. I didn't want to go grocery shopping with him. I didn't want to help decorate his apartment. I didn't want to meet his family. I wanted to kiss him, make him laugh, suck him off, go for drinks, joke around, but mostly I wanted to fuck. A lot.

I could tell he was scared. Scared of breaking up my marriage. He was naïve, but handsome.

After two pints we walked to his place. He made some jokes, said that I looked like a lesbian. I was fine with that, since I did like women too.

His roommate was home. Eating a bagel in the kitchen. We talked for a minute. I'd seen him at a few parties, so I knew him a little. I knew he didn't approve of us seeing each other but didn't care enough to try to prevent it. I didn't want to intrude. I went to the bathroom, let them talk for a few minutes. I'd remembered it different somehow. I'd thrown up there a few weeks before. I'd been sure there were wood floors, that the toilet was across from the sink.

The roommate was gone when I came out.

We went to his room. He put on some music. I leaned down to look at his books. He grabbed me by the waist and pulled me toward the bed. I wanted him, and I could see that he wanted me too, but that he was still scared. We kissed. He was a good kisser. It was more tender than I expected. He talked a lot. He said: who do you belong to?

I found the question strange, but endearing, as if he didn't want to take something that wasn't his to take. I said: I belong to me.

I was naked. He looked me over. He said: you're the most feminine girl I've ever been with.

He was naked too. He was still soft. He seemed anxious. I knew he was thinking about my husband. I heard him say under his breath: I should have quit.

I said: why?

He said: because I don't want to run into your husband at the bookstore.

He kissed my hands. He sucked on my fingertips. He said: when we're at work together and you go into your office, I count the minutes until you come back.

I liked his presence, being there with him. Even though I could tell the sex would be tame. I liked the way he touched me. The way he looked at me.

Neither of us came that night. It was hard for me to leave his arms. Before I went home, I slipped Hubert Aquin's *The Invention of Death* under his bed. He had never read it. I thought he'd like it. He reminded me of the main character.

I let myself out the back door and called a taxi. It was the middle of November.

::

I'd invited him to the party for the book fair. I'd insisted he come. He showed up with his roommate. That was fine. It meant I wouldn't have to entertain him. I was drunk. I'd set myself a limit. The week before, I'd been out of control, had thrown up and passed out on the floor.

We danced. Toward the end of the night, we were standing around a high table, leaning in close as we talked. We didn't really know what we were doing. I was attracted to him, but I wasn't sure. He said: you're married.

I said: that's not the problem. The problem is that I'm your boss.

He said: you're telling me it's not a problem for your husband.

I said: exactly.

He said: it's work?

I said: yes.

He kissed me. I wasn't expecting it, but I was happy. So happy. We kept kissing, for more than twenty minutes, all over each other like a couple of teenagers. I shivered every time he brushed a finger over my nipples. A poet friend came by and said: you're not doing anything stupid, are you?

I said: no.

She said: do you need me to rescue you?

I said: no.

We laughed. We kissed some more. I was working the next day. I had to go home. I ran into my publisher as I stumbled toward the door. We said goodnight. I knew I had a dumb smile on my face. I felt sixteen again. My publisher said: are you okay to get home?

I said: yes.

::

The arrangement with my husband was simple but necessary for the survival of an open marriage. The other relationships couldn't harm our own. No falling in love or sleeping over. We had to choose people outside of our circle. There was a list of forbidden names. The list I made for him was longer. Probably because I had more of a jealous streak. For the moment, it was working.

I was the one who'd brought it up. Guillaume had often mentioned it in the past, but I wasn't ready. I'd had bad experiences. I kind of knew how it went. I was reluctant. Guillaume liked to sleep with men, so when I wanted to see other men too, he said yes.

We had an active sex life. It was still nice. Entertaining enough. We planned to spend our lives together. We told ourselves we should enjoy our bodies now while we were young. And what were a few lovers in a lifetime spent together?

::

I arrived at his place a bit late. But not unreasonably so. He was in a bad mood for some reason. I'd had the dumb idea of taking half a speed pill before coming over. I was falling asleep and wanted to wake myself up, but it just made me anxious. I didn't want him to know. We crossed the street to the bar. We sat in a booth, side by side like Europeans. I liked that image. Our knees were touching. I kept faltering. I was having trouble keeping the conversation going. My throat felt tight. I ended up telling him that I'd taken something. He laughed. That probably fit the picture he had of me. He ordered for me. It gave me a kind of thrill. I wanted to be that for him, a submissive little thing. A submissive little thing who would drink whatever he chose. The beer calmed me down a bit. We talked. I said: what do you want out of life?

He paused, didn't answer right away. I said: what do you want to happen? Tell me about your dreams.

He said: for now, I want a better job. And I want to make something out of what I have. (I think he was talking about doing something creative. About writing.) I want to enjoy being young. I want to spend time with my friends.

His beer was disappearing faster than mine. I was spending too much time swallowing and shifting my jaw back and forth because of the speed.

He turned to me and said: when I kiss you, you change. Your voice changes. Your whole demeanor changes. It's fascinating.

He didn't kiss me because I changed the subject. I felt self-conscious. We finished our drinks. I paid. It was easier that way. We went across to his place. His roommate was listening to music. We talked to him for a bit. I laid my coat on the same chair as the other times. I said: look, I'm starting to develop habits.

He said: don't do that.

I laughed. We opened the bottle of wine I'd brought. He got himself a beer. We went into his room. He put on some music. I sat on the bed. He came and sat next to me. We kissed. I liked his tongue, his lips. He ran his hands up my thighs. He said: you're beautiful.

I didn't say anything. I kissed him and lay back on the bed. He grabbed my legs and lifted them up to rest on his shoulders. We stayed like that talking for a while. He said: so how does this work?

I said: what do you mean?

He said: do you tell each other? You know, "By the way, I slept with this girl last week."

I said: no, we tell each other beforehand. He knows I'm with you.

Henry Lee by PJ Harvey and Nick Cave came on. I loved that song. I finished my glass of wine. He went to get me another. I lay down on my back. He balanced the glass on my forehead. I didn't move. He bent to kiss me, the glass still in place. He poured wine into my mouth then kissed me. The cold wine, his hot tongue. The taste. I was getting drunk. My head was spinning. I hadn't eaten dinner, and probably had very little for lunch. I said: I don't feel well.

He pulled the wastepaper basket closer. I went to the bathroom. I looked like shit. I went back to the bedroom. I said: I didn't get sick.

He pulled back the covers. I lay down and fell asleep.

Two hours later he said: it's late. You really can't stay over?

I said: no.

I looked at my phone. It was already past five. I tried to get up but I was too comfortable. We kissed. I wanted him. I wanted to fuck him, to have him inside me. I felt foggy. Too messed up to have sex. I said: I don't know anymore where I end and you begin. It's like we're the same thing.

I managed to get myself out of bed. I got dressed and I said: you're so handsome.

He smiled. I said: don't get up. I'll call a taxi.

I went outside and waited on the sidewalk. It was snowing. The taxi pulled up.

The next day I read this sentence in the Claire Legendre novel: "All that could be done was to sink into sleep, between two halves of a man that formed a single untouchable phantom."

::

I was cat-sitting at a friend's apartment for two days. It worked out well for her, and for me too since it was right next to the bookstore. I'd invited him to come over after his shift. He'd hesitated, nervous. But then he said yes. I wasn't sure he'd come. He showed up at five thirty. He came in and looked around the apartment. He was curious. I offered him a beer and he took one. He seemed happy. I guess I'd made the right choice at the corner store. The heat was off in every room but the bedroom. We were in the living room, wrapped in a blanket. We talked. He'd had dinner with his family the night before. He told me stories about his sisters, their difficult teenage years. Familiar stories. It was charming, the idea that he might understand my faults and failings. He was really close to them as a kid. He'd slept in their beds, kept their secrets, consoled them. He'd wanted to fight all the boys who broke their hearts. I could tell his sisters were powerful figures in his world. They'd influenced his relationships with women. We finished our beers. I went to get two more. He went to the bathroom. I decided we should move to the bedroom. My fingers were stiff with cold. He came out of the bathroom. I was waiting on the bed. He looked around the room. He picked up a few things and commented on them, telling me the ways my friends were different from his. My friends left almonds on their nightstand, covered their router with tinfoil, kept forty identical keys on the same keychain, had a teabag tree (ten years of used teabags on a calendar rack). The cat wandered in. We kissed. Then got undressed. Then I'm not sure what. Hands, mouths. I had condoms in my bag. He took one out. He'd always blow into it before putting it on.

He slowly pushed inside me. He stopped to go to the bathroom. When he came back he said:

mm, I think you're bleeding. There was blood on the condom.

I checked, and I was. I grabbed some tissue. I looked at the sheets. They were fine. I said: you've torn me all up.

He said: you must have gotten your period.

I said: no. Wait, pass me my computer.

I opened the calendar. I counted. I said: that's not possible.

We started kissing again. He was afraid of hurting me so he turned me over instead. I was starting to realize he didn't like condoms. When we had anal sex, he didn't always wear one. I said: come in my ass.

And he did. Then we lay there holding each other. He had plans, had to be home around eight. It was maybe seven thirty. He didn't seem to care. I said: why did you ask me if I could handle pain?

He said: I don't know.

I said: well I can. You can hurt me.

He said: I'm scared I'd like it too much.

I said: please.

He kissed me. He grabbed my jaw and slapped me. Then sat on top of me and put his hands around my throat. I could still manage a bit of air. He held me there for a long time. Then he let go. He stopped and started seven or eight times. My legs were trembling, spasming. Each time he released his grip, I took a gulp of air. I could see in his eyes that he liked seeing me that way. He gritted his teeth. His cock was hard. He brought his face close to mine and he said: don't die.

I didn't want him to ever let me go. I wanted to believe he could kill me. I wanted him to stay there gripping my neck for years until I slipped away forever. He said: you belong to me. Look at me.

I looked at him, into his green eyes. Then he squeezed hard. I thought he must love me a little.

He left around ten. The next day, he told me he wished he'd stayed at least another hour. I was happy.

::

I was attracted to him from the first time we met. He'd transferred from another store just before I left on unpaid leave. I'd gotten a grant to work on a collection of poetry and I wanted to focus on writing. I thought he was really funny. I spent a lot of time talking with him. And because I was leaving, I was laid-back at work, I joked around,

I didn't really care. He seemed fascinated by the fact that I wrote (and had been published). We texted sometimes over the summer. He'd catch me up on bookstore news, ask how my manuscript was coming along. I came back to work in the fall and we reconnected right away. We'd open the store together on Sunday mornings. We spent more time talking than working. One day, I invited him over to do mushrooms. We spent the night staring at our hands and laughing. I asked if he wanted to stay over. He didn't get that I wanted to sleep with him. I was married. At that time, he didn't know anything about our arrangement. He went home. I slept alone. Guillaume was in Quebec City for an art opening.

One night, I dreamed I was driving him to the airport. I saw him off. We lay down in the parking lot to kiss for the first and last time. I said to him: you're finally here.

He said: I was always here.

Then we became two cubic shapes, coloured and pixelated. Like a kind of gas. Maybe it was a physical representation of how I saw the soul. As we drew closer, we started to dissolve. We cancelled each other out and disappeared.

I ended up explaining the agreement with my husband. We started sleeping together two weeks later.

::

I wrote.

::

I found it easy, being with two men at once. I had my husband and I had my lover. I felt no guilt. I wasn't lying to either of them. I kept some details to myself, but I didn't lie. My lover often said to me: there's no way your husband isn't jealous.

I loved it when he said that. It showed that what we were doing meant something to him. I'd say: he's not jealous at all, it's not in his nature.

I liked the balancing act, the work the situation required. I had to cloak the truth so that each felt indispensable. It was easy, because they were. They were indispensable to me.

::

I got to the bar first, the same one as usual. I recognized the server. I'd met her at a party where once again, I'd cried, thrown up, made a fool of myself. She'd washed my face, rinsed my hair.

I went to sit at the bar, far from her. I was embarrassed. He walked in. He saw me right away, didn't have to look. He took off his coat. He was wearing a blazer underneath. I found that weird. A blazer on a Tuesday night. I said: you wore a blazer. He said: yes, to impress you. Now I can take it off.

He draped it over the back of his chair. I'd already ordered a pint. He ordered the same. The bar was packed. We drank. There was a hockey game on. He wasn't paying attention to it. We ordered more beers. On the way to the bathroom, I said hi to the server. I was starting to get drunk so was feeling less shy. We chatted a little. She said: if you get sick tonight, I'll be here.

I laughed. She added: your hair will be easier to wash now that it's shorter.

I laughed again, then went to the bathroom.

I felt drunk and nervous. I'd shredded my coaster. He was telling me about a girl. He had a tendency to talk about other girls. It annoyed me a bit. We ordered more drinks. I didn't feel well. I made a few bad jokes to the server. We left, went over to his place. His roommate wasn't there. We sat in the living room. I was in a bad mood. I thought about leaving the room, or even the apartment. I remembered that Guillaume had someone over. Leaving would have been complicated. Where would I go? A hotel? A friend's place? I didn't have a choice. I stayed.

He ended up bringing me to his room. We fucked. I slept there.

::

I'd closed the bookstore and run to buy beer. I got to his place around twenty to eleven. Same as always.

::

We were careful to keep our distance from one another that night. It was the staff Christmas party.

We took a taxi to his place after. We went in, talked a little. He started fingering me. I was tired. Him too, even if he didn't want to admit it. I told him it could wait till morning. He nodded. We fell asleep entwined.

I woke up first. I slipped on a cardigan from his closet and went to the bathroom. I came back. He kissed my forehead. We went back to sleep for another hour or two. I had to work at three. I needed to go home, to shower and change. I'd told my husband I'd be back early. I had an application to finish for Wednesday. I tried to drag myself out of bed, but I couldn't. I wanted to stay there too badly, wanted his arms, his mouth. He straddled my chest. I touched myself. I came. He came on my face, in my mouth, still choking me. Time slipped by.

We lay in each other's arms a long time. I wanted more, I think he did too. I had to leave. His arms were still around me, his eyes on mine. I finally got up. I took a taxi. I showered. Headed back to the bookstore. He texted me: come back.

I responded: I'm coming.

That night, he sent me poems. I found it sweet.

::

The novel was starting to go in circles. We were repeating ourselves. Always the same order of events drawing us together: the kisses, the embraces, a mouth on a neck, a hand on an ass, the clothes we'd strip off, the caresses, fingers, mouths, nipples. The violence was escalating but even that wasn't enough. There were still no feelings, no attachment, no drama in sight. Just sex and a few slaps.

::

The launch had ended at seven. I had three hours to kill before meeting him. I was in a bar in Plaza Saint-Hubert. I'd ordered an IPA. I was reading, trying to write. After my beer, I went to the drug-store, wandered through the aisles, bought tooth-paste, makeup remover wipes. Then I left for his place. I still had a lot of time. I walked instead of taking the bus. He still wasn't home, so I went for another beer at the bar across the street. He showed up, ordered a drink. We watched the girls at the next table. Made up stories about their lives, assigned them professions. He had his arm around me. I felt like a teenager.

At his place, we talked to his roommate. We each drank a glass of water. Lay down in bed.

Music. Clothes off. Finger. Mouth.

Condom. My pussy. *Henry Lee*. No condom. My ass.

I come. He comes.

Kiss on the forehead. A shared banana.

He said: I almost came with the condom on. That hasn't happened in years.

I smiled. We slept close. I woke up before him. Bathroom. Bed. Asleep. Awake again. Kisses. Finger. Mouth. Clit. His knee on my chest. No air. His hands around my throat. His cum in my mouth. More kisses. A long time in his arms.

I suggested we go out for breakfast. I mostly wanted a coffee. We got dressed. He looked at the time. Two o'clock. He said: it's a bit late for breakfast.

He walked me to the door. I said: sorry for staying so long.

He said: stop.

We kissed. I left. I went to buy blackberries and a bottle of Perrier. I cried as I walked to the metro.

::

We never did buy plane tickets for Prague. I'd wanted to believe it. We had no plans for the future. We had no future. All we had was a red room on Beaubien.

::

I'd told a friend that I wanted to start seeing an employee. He'd said: go for it. It's your chance to have some fun with the object of your desire.

I was thinking of sending my manuscript to this same friend, once it was done, to see what he thought. I valued his opinion. I knew he wouldn't hold back. He'd tell me what I didn't want to hear. He always did. So I had to write more. The Word document had to grow. It was moving slowly.

::

Long before we started sleeping together, we'd seen each other at a poetry launch. It was while I was on leave to write. I hadn't seen him in maybe two months. He was with a friend from work who published with the same press as I did. I was happy to run into them. I kissed my friend hello. To him, I said: I don't know you well enough. Just shake my hand.

I had taken mushrooms the day before. I'd gone to the salon with a friend, a manicure for her heartbreak. It was cliché, but it had worked. I had inch-long purple nails, filed to a point. I was wearing platforms, a long skirt, a ripped t-shirt. I felt good, vibrant and confident. The launch was at my publisher's apartment. I'd had a few drinks. I was fighting with a friend. Our publisher separated us when we started hitting each other with chairs. I liked fighting with boys. I wanted to be in their club. I wanted to be a poet, not a female poet.

The guests disappeared one by one, heading off to other parties. He lived next door. I was hoping he'd invite me for a last drink at his place, even if I couldn't have gone. Leaving the party, we kissed on both cheeks. He said: now we know each other well enough.

Already, I was interested.

::

He didn't answer my messages, just came straight over. He knocked on my apartment door. He'd managed to get in behind another tenant. I was just getting out of the shower. I hadn't had time to clean up. The dishes were piled beside the sink, my hair was wet, I was embarrassed. He knocked again. I threw on a long shirt. I texted him: just a minute. I'm coming.

I picked up my dirty underwear, closed the bedroom door, ran to let him in. He stood at the door, handsome, but unsure. He didn't look like a man overcome with the wild desire to fuck me. I invited him in. I offered him a beer. We went into my office. He said: I feel weird. Are you sure your husband isn't going to come home?

I said: don't worry. He won't be back till ten.

He looked at the art on the wall. He stopped talking every time the pipes creaked. I put on music. We kissed. That was always my favourite part. His mouth. His lips. His tongue. Before long, I was on top of him. I came quickly.

I screamed. I was embarrassed. I said: do you want me to suck your dick?

He said: yes.

He stayed there on the couch. I knelt down on the rug. He came in my mouth. I rested my head on his thigh and looked up at him. His eyes, his face. His cock, still swollen. He looked good. I said: you're gorgeous.

He smiled and said: my head is spinning.

I was happy to have that effect on him. We watched YouTube videos. Talked a little. Then he left.

::

We had room 43. The hotel was sketchy. For forty-two dollars with tax, you couldn't really expect much more. I said to the receptionist: I thought it was more than that.

He said: Madame, usually people don't complain when it's cheaper than expected.

I flashed him a fake smile. I went upstairs, to a room out of a David Lynch film. It was big, the space poorly used. There wasn't much furniture. Everything was worn. A light was blinking on the telephone. I picked up the receiver. Nothing. I put my things down next to the bed, took out my computer, moved the chair and the night-

33

stand, put on music. I poured myself a plastic cup of wine.

I waited an hour for him to get there. He inspected the room. He laughed. He was like a kid. He turned up the heat. We made love. We fell asleep. The bed was huge. We slept on opposite sides. We woke up. We made love again. We talked for a while. He had a cold.

It was daylight on Avenue du Parc. He left the room before me. We were near the bookstore and still afraid our coworkers might see us together. I watched him walking ahead of me for a long time. I followed his brown leather jacket through the crowd. He turned onto Laurier. I lost him. I went to the grocery store and bought a litre of kombucha and some veggie pâté. I went home. I ate a piece of toast. I made a cup of tea. I tried to write. I read instead.

::

Our story was falling flat. All of this waiting for a few euphoric moments, it was exhausting. The moments came, but not often enough. I didn't want to hold back. I wanted to throw myself into it. Set everything on fire. Be with him, be crazy. I felt like we were going to run out of time. He was afraid of getting close, becoming attached, being a couple. He was solitary, had a full inner life. Once a week was the deal. No more. He didn't want to lose control. I knew he'd let me into his life because I wasn't a threat. A married woman, the ideal arrangement. He was holding me at a distance, but other times felt so close. Closer than anyone had been. Closer than I'd imagined possible.

::

We'd been arguing that week. Communicating by text complicated everything. He seemed distant. I didn't get his sense of humour. I ended up calling him while I was in the bath. I was kind of sad. I wanted him to just magically understand. I didn't want to feel insistent, or needy. I just wanted us to have fun. I needed to feel something, anything, whatever that was. Not even love, just any emotion to make me feel at least a little alive. I needed it. He thought I was being demanding. I probably was. Being with him was a drug, and coming down was hard.

I swallowed down my desires.

It was one of the worst nights of that winter. I lay in my office, tears and snot pouring. I cupped a handful of pills. I cried for a long time. I couldn't move. It wasn't him. It was everything else. It was winter. A dark season that brought all my dark thoughts to the surface. I thought about the book. I wanted to finish it. Just to write it. It lifted me out of my depression a little, gave me hope.

I woke up on Monday around noon. I squeezed a grapefruit, poured glasses of juice for myself and my husband. I wanted to stop. I wanted it just to be us again. We talked about it over toast. I cried a little, thinking of the novel. I would have nothing to write about anymore. I wanted to abandon the project. He said I should keep going. He was so empathetic. I knew our marriage was strong and would endure. He was the only one who understood my writing process. I don't know if I'd ever loved him more, my giant.

::

I'd never experienced the emotions of those early days of a new relationship. I'd always dated my best friends. Never a stranger. It was all new, the flirting, the excitement of first messages, first looks, first kisses. Discovering a person as I discovered their body.

I felt good about myself. I had jumped into something. I'd never felt so young. I scrawled his name on bathroom walls. I hid in the closet to talk to him on the phone. I had a secret lover.

Keeping each other a secret added a shimmer of excitement. There were a lot of close calls. We texted about it for hours, looking for better ways to hide. It brought us closer. Our hands constantly running over each other's thighs, backs, necks. We knew we'd eventually give ourselves away.

And then there was this other employee who was becoming friends with his roommate. That complicated things. I was afraid my boss would find out, that I'd lose my job. I didn't want to be transferred to Laval with no choice but to accept, since February wasn't a great month to be looking for a job.

::

I'd had, up till then, a fairly binary idea of sexuality. I'd been in a relationship with a woman, then with my husband. There'd been things in between, but almost always in the context of a party, drinking. Nothing long term. So, nothing. My sexual experience had mostly been shaped by the two of them. Without really realizing it, I'd categorized practices according to gender. The way a woman touched, the way a man did.

I found out this was wrong. That there was only the way a person touches and gender didn't have much to do with the way we are with one another.

At the same time, this was the longest I'd ever slept with a straight man.

I'd never loved a straight man before.

::

The Wednesday shift. That was usually our day together. I'd be finishing my work week; he'd be starting his. It was the only day neither of us had to work the next morning.

Thursday morning, I'd go home. I'd eat with my husband. We'd talk about our nights. I'd make a pot of tea. I'd sit in front of my computer and transcribe what had happened the day before. Then I could move on to other things.

::

I was going to Brussels for the book fair. He'd made me a list of places I should go. He'd spent a few days there in the fall.

I got a message from him before takeoff. It said: bye beautiful, xxx.

38

I smiled. I opened my book. My bookmark was a list of films that had made him cry. I'd forgotten I'd put it there. I read the list again. I took a photo of it to send him. In Brussels, I thought of him at every street corner. I imagined him stopping to check the map, buying a waffle, taking a photo. The first night, I wrote him: I wish you were here with me. I found us the perfect life.

I wrote in my notebook: The Cure – Guerre Froide – Kraftwerk, I'd like to live here with you. It was made for us. A red bar.

I fell in love with Brussels, with the energy of the city. I'd been worried about the weather, the grey, but in the end it suited me and my melancholic nature.

I stayed out late with the other authors who were there for the fair. I barely slept. I was constantly drunk. I was soaring. One night I'd been drinking and I wrote him: my novel will be called *Goodnight, Sébastien*. Halfway through, it's going to become surrealist autofiction. I'll turn into a mermaid and live in the Brussels Canal.

He laughed. At least, that's what I understood from his message.

::

We'd arranged to meet in the early evening. He was supposed to come join me. I spent a long time getting ready. I did my hair. I couldn't decide between the ponytail that made me look young or a low knot. I decided to leave it loose on my shoulders. A wave along my cheek. He showed up a little late, smiling. I was smiling too. We hadn't seen each other in two weeks. He came over to me. I was wearing a backless dress that showed off my tattoo. Between my shoulder blades, a snake curled around the moon, swallowing its own tail. A souvenir from my travels in South America. My grandmother had been startled when she first saw it, the ouroboros over my heart chakra. She saw more significance in it than I did.

He slid his hand over my back right away and said: you have such soft skin. I know women almost always do, but yours is unusually soft.

I smiled. We stood up. I was having trouble walking. I was a mermaid with legs. They'd told me that the pain would only last for a few hours. I would get used to the feeling of the ground beneath my feet. We went to a bar he liked. He kept running his hand up and down my back, his

40

fingers tracing the seam of my dress, trying to uncover more skin. He ordered two beers. Mine tasted of cherries. It was delicious. I listened to the music playing, cold wave, atmospheric. The tables around us ceased to exist. I looked at him. Green eyes, full lower lip. I reached for his ear, brushed my fingers along it. We were both starting to get drunk.

We walked to his hotel. My legs were already working better. I lost my balance a couple of times at most. He caught me, held me up. My unsteadiness was endearing, gave him an excuse to touch me. We went into the room. I lay down on the bed. We melted into each other. I had no regrets about trading my voice for these legs and what was between them. He entered me. We fucked. Hard. Long. Then slept. Hand in hand. Forehead to forehead. Like old lovers. Still entwined.

I wondered: could a mermaid without a voice still write? Maybe that's all she could do. Not speak, just write and offer up her body.

In the morning I got dressed. He was waking up. I pointed to the door. He understood I had to go.

He said: you can go, but leave your mouth here with me.

I nodded.

I had a pussy. I had a voice in my writing. What good was a mouth?

::

I knew the Andersen tale before the Disney movie. This spurred my first literary debates at school, because in my version the mermaid dies. To die for love. Already, at six, this seemed valid, logical, even desirable. I learned that love never ends well, that nobody gets married and lives happily ever after. You have to suffer, end up as sea foam. And I was ready for it.

I got older and there were good relationships, and even those that ended badly didn't leave me too bitter. I respected my exes. Or my ex, as she was the only one worth mentioning. We'd talk a few times a month. We were still close despite the distance.

I was still wrestling with that romantic idea of love. I was ready to give myself over. I wanted to feel love like that, compromise myself, burn myself to the ground.

::

I'd been back from Brussels for three days. I was waiting for him at the bar. He came in before I'd had a chance to order. He was smiling when he came in. I couldn't help smiling back. I was so excited to see him. We talked about my trip, about travelling, beer, all kinds of things. We hurried across the street to his place to make love. We fell asleep.

In the morning, we picked up where we'd left off. He touched me. He gripped my neck. I liked to push his cock down my throat as far as possible and keep it there a long time without breathing. Then I'd come up for air. He'd choke me. When he saw I couldn't take any more, he'd let go and hold me against his chest. There was a cadence to it. It was all orchestrated right up to the moment when he came and I came too. That morning was the same, except maybe we wanted to go further, to do more, because we'd missed each other. After many rounds of this, he let go and I started hyperventilating. He gave me some space. We didn't panic. I managed to slow my breathing until I stopped completely. He leaned over me and said: breathe.

I was frozen. Lulled into torpor. He shook me. I took a breath. Not even a breath. Barely anything, a tiny sip of air, just enough to let me dive back in. I lay motionless on the bed, sinking into the black. Worry on his face. He shook me again. Nothing. I didn't really want to come back. The world was calm and quiet from where I lay. He brought his ear to my mouth. Nothing. No warmth, no breath. His features blurred, his eyes disappeared. He grabbed my shoulders and shook me. Again. Then again. Then I started breathing.

::

I'd been depressed for days, and I couldn't see clearly anymore. I knew I didn't have the will to be happy. I knew it wasn't important to me. This story only made sense when I was writing it. If I didn't write for a week, I started thinking I was in love, on the brink of divorce. I needed to pour everything onto the page. When I finished a good paragraph, none of the rest mattered, my pain, my loss, my guilt. There was the text. It would save me. It would allow everything to exist, even me. That was a large part of the project. I'd noticed that during my anxiety attacks, I turned to Facebook to validate my existence. There I could find proof of myself. I had photos, a certain number of friends classified by category; I had interests and conversations. It was so reassuring to feel present in the world. There's a record of me, I exist. And I could also say: I have a book, I exist. It validated my pain, rendered it necessary.

::

My husband's bisexuality no longer worried me. It had made me anxious in the past. Sometimes really anxious. But opening our relationship seemed to have killed my fear of him cheating. My fear of him lying. I knew what was going on. It was right there, laid out in front of me. Our arrangement quelled my anxiety. Before, I was afraid of having to compete with men. With women, it was at least a fair fight. With a man, I had nothing. I'd detested them. Hated them. They had weapons I knew nothing of.

And then, this idea of the bisexual with the wandering eye is ridiculous. I was bisexual myself. I hadn't been with a woman in years and I was doing fine.

Rationally, I knew I could trust him, but sometimes the anxiety won out. Doubts and misunderstandings fed the monster. Male bisexuality has the dangerous quality of being difficult to understand, or believe. Nobody ever questions a homosexual relationship in a woman's life, while a man

45

is automatically in the closet. It took me a while
to understand this.

::

All my ideas about sex were being dismantled.
I thought I'd understood it. I mean, not the
practice of it but the emotions. I thought I'd
loved, desired, but I was realizing that it could
be different.

::

There were moments of panic too. I wondered who my body belonged to. I had to make
compromises to accommodate everyone who
wanted it: my lover, my husband. But I was
the one putting pressure on myself, not them.
I had to let them do what they wanted or lose
them. And why was losing them so terrifying?
What did it matter in the end? I was scared of
not having anyone. I was scared of being alone.
I was scared of never feeling happiness again.
I wanted them both. I wanted them differently,
but equally. To keep them for myself. To have
them within reach, tame them, hold onto them
forever. I knew it wouldn't last. Spring was
coming. Things would shift. I sank down into
the sofa and tried to write poems. I listened to

music, sometimes I cried. Tears, then an Ativan. My mind would quiet, leave me calm with the blank pages of my notebook. The same songs played on loop, but I couldn't write anymore.

::

We decided to get married in April 2013. Guillaume had been in Paris all fall. It was a difficult period. I found the distance hard. We nearly broke up. Empty boxes sat in the kitchen waiting to be filled. In the end I went to meet him. I spent two weeks with him in his studio in Paris. A kind of romance outside of time. Before I took the plane home, I had an anxiety attack. And then another in Montreal on the expressway. Coming home hadn't been easy for him either. We had to reconnect. January and February were awful. We were locked into a kind of psychosis, spiralling downward. I was probably depressed. I stopped leaving the house. I was afraid of taking public transportation. I barely worked anymore, was always on the verge of hiding in the closet. He tried to be supportive, but didn't really understand what I was going through. Time went by and nothing much changed. Then, one night in March, we went out. The wind was high, but it wasn't cold. We walked to the metro, then to the mineralogy centre. We'd finally left the stifling apartment, gotten away from the knife marks on the walls. It was a beautiful night among the minerals and rocks. We were happy.

We were already engaged, even though we had no solid plans. He'd bought me a ring for my birthday the year before, a simple gold band. He'd said something like: maybe this means we'll get married. If you want.

I found it sweet. I remember coming harder looking at the ring. I knew I was ridiculous. Maybe this would mean I couldn't be abandoned so easily.

April, the announcement. The wedding in August. Just a few guests, a small ceremony organized by a couple of friends, a beautiful party, flowers and wine.

::

I had to put myself at risk, since that was all I had left, since I didn't really care about anything, since I didn't love life enough to want to be good at it. And since I was here in this world, I figured I might as well fuck everything up, cry my heart out, slog through my days, constantly on the edge of the abyss. Writing was a way to validate the human experience, a necessity before the absurdity of existence.

Was I a hypocrite to say I was doing this just to write about it, to bring everything back to the novel, to put writing before desire? Because the desire was there, answering to its own logic and needing no rational justification. Was I only writing this book to escape my guilt? My guilt at falling in love with another man, breaking my promise, finding myself as disloyal as anyone else.

::

We'd banked on our image as the perfect couple for a long time. They called us "The Adjutors" because of Guillaume's name. My name was overwritten. I was lost next to him, the talented one. At the time, this suited me just fine. I hadn't done anything, apart from selling photocopied poems for two dollars in a few church basements. So we were the Adjutors. I did everything I could to fulfill the requirements of this position. After the wedding, we became a couple people would look to. The only one in our circle of friends that was still going strong. Once, around a campfire, I'd even overheard a friend

say: look at them. We all know marriage, relationships... But it seems like they could make it
work.

And now, we'd known each other for years, we
had a strong friendship as a foundation, similar
interests, an intellectual connection. We were
perfect.

Eventually, I wanted a baby. I wanted to be
the ideal mother. A natural birth, a breastfed
diaper-free baby, alternative parenting, home-
schooling, 24/7. I imagined the perfect child.
What else could we possibly have?
    We tried for a little while. Guillaume didn't
seem fully invested in the idea, and then we
were supposed to go to Switzerland. No way to
give birth there, not practical to be seven months
pregnant. So we stopped. I decided not to try
again. We wouldn't be parents, that wouldn't be
us. I changed my mind, closed that door. One
less decision to make, one road we wouldn't go
down. The end of something. Our first end.

::

I hated not having time with him. Our sched-
ules barely aligned. We'd often meet up around

eleven at night. We'd have till the morning. Time raced by. Thursday, when I'd leave, I'd have to wait an entire week before I was in his arms again. I forgot the things I wanted to say to him, do to him. I dreamed of a trip. Even just two days. Barely anything. Just a little more than what we had. I was still dreaming of Prague. An apartment in Lisbon. Brussels, where we would have been happy. A road trip around the Gaspé Peninsula. I was waiting.

::

We left work together. We took my usual route home. I told him all the things I'd been thinking of that week. I was happy. We stopped under the dome at Square-Victoria station. I loved the acoustics of that spot. I told him how I'd heard a man singing opera there once. Our footsteps echoed. We went to buy condoms, stopped to eat. Continued on to my apartment. We drank a beer, watched videos online. We fucked on the couch in my office. I was on top. Clinging to him. Our skin hot. I held onto his neck, shouted his name. I had a first orgasm, long and gentle. I felt calm. He wanted to give me another, so I let him. Then I don't know what happened. I started hyperventilating again. But this time,

I panicked, not understanding what was happening. I started to cry. I cried on his shoulder without him even realizing, my heavy breathing drowning out the sound. Then I stopped breathing altogether. For a long time. The same feeling as before, but more intense. I felt doubled: a physical body in shock and a spirit floating, far above in the darkness. Two disconnected forms.

In the days that followed, I stayed at home alone in the apartment. I was a disaster.

: :

I erased certain details about my life.

: :

I was almost thirty. I actually wasn't even sure anymore. I'd been lying about my age for a long time. I was between twenty-six and twenty-nine. It made me panic, the thought of time passing. I was afraid of not being somebody. And all I had was writing. Writing that would save me in the end, this novel I wanted to finish, so I'd at least have two. Two novels, a book of poems and another posthumous collection. Maybe that would make me a writer, a little something.

Nothing was going well. I stopped eating, lost twenty-five pounds over the winter. I was stricken with panic attacks.

I expected him to save me, to take me out of myself. Winter dragged on.

::

I'd picked out some clothes. Ugly ones. I didn't want to make the effort to be pretty. I had dirty hair, makeup smudged under my eyes. I'd had anal sex with my lover that morning. I'd fucked my husband that night. I had my period. I stank. I took my pill container, filled it with what was left of the Ativan and Dilaudid from the bathroom cabinet and put it in my left coat pocket, my phone in the other. I took a bottle of water. I told my husband I was going for a walk. He asked if I was coming back. I said: yes.

I went out. I ended up at the edge of the canal just next to the Mill bridge. The snow crunched under my feet. I thought the ice would have thawed already. I walked under the bridge. I heard the water flowing between the gates of the lock. I went closer. Almost nothing, a trickle. Ten feet below. No way to get down. I thought about jumping. This wasn't how I'd imagined it. I kept walking. Still no way to get to the water. I stopped to write. I wanted to leave one last poem. I didn't really know what I was doing anymore. It was cold. I could have stayed sitting there, waiting for the pills to put me to sleep. I hadn't considered how the Ativan would mix with the Dilaudid. I'd mostly thought about slipping into hypothermia. I'd stolen the idea of the canal from Claire Legendre: "You let yourself fall in, like that swan the other morning, the dead swan washed up on the banks." It was clever. A canal in Prague, a canal in Montreal. I walked on. I tried to slip down the side of a footbridge but it was too high. I turned back. I left the bottle of water in a snowbank. I walked back to the apartment, watching my feet. I rang the buzzer. I didn't have my keys. I didn't think I'd need them again. My husband opened the door and I went in. I put the pill container away in my nightstand. I sat in front of the computer. I put on *Going to a Town* by Rufus Wainwright. I cried.

::

He was sitting in my office. He spent nearly all his breaks there. We were talking about his insomnia. I said: I want to save you.

54

He said: I've never known anyone who wanted to save me as much as you do.

I said: maybe I'll manage to.

::

I'd packed a rope in my bag. We were in his hometown, out with his friends. We were drinking beer. His ex at the end of the table. I couldn't really see what the connection could be between us. I tried not to think about it too much. We were waiting on another round. I said to him: I have a surprise for you. Look in my bag.

He smiled, more taken aback than happy, when he saw the long black rope. Our beers came. We stayed at the bar late, then drove back to Montreal with his roommate and two friends. He put on Les Cowboys Fringants in the car. I hadn't listened to them in years. I rested my head on his shoulder. I thought about my ex, her cancer, my friends from that time who I barely saw anymore. I felt so alone, overwhelmed by the feeling that I'd never have anyone. People passed through my life. He would move on too. My husband already had. Why get attached all over again?

At the apartment, we talked a little. It was late. I was on top of him. He had the rope. I'd studied a few bondage ties. He seemed surprised by my ease, asked if I'd done this often. It was the first time. The rope went around my neck, a first knot over my breasts, a second beneath them and a third lower down. Then over my pussy, my ass, back up to my neck, where the two ends separated and passed through each of the knots in front again. We fucked like that. He came. We slept late, like teenagers, until one o'clock.

::

I wanted to learn how to live alone. I'd never done it. I'd always taken elaborate care to avoid solitude. I'd been single for two months over ten years. Almost never slept alone. I'd built relationships just to have someone, and I'd had sex for the same reason.

At that point, I thought I had to choose between my marriage and my novel. I had to totally commit to one or the other. The novel demanded I go further, be alone, always more alone. And I had nothing else, only writing could still save my skin. If I kept trying to write the book without making any compromises in my life, the story would fall flat. Another banal record of heartbreak. Why did I believe so strongly that I needed to write? Why was it so important? Because it was saving me. That verb again. It was important because it took over everything. Because it forced me to ruin myself for a better story. Maybe that was cheating. But I was the one making the rules. I was the queen here in the country of my novel.

I told Guillaume I needed to be alone. A first step. We agreed on a few days. He went to his parents' place. It wasn't enough. I wanted to move, to find an empty room, live there with nothing but a mattress on the floor, a rug, my computer, headphones and a bookshelf. I'd leave him everything else. I saw it as a test. I would break myself into pieces. I knew I wouldn't be able to do it, wouldn't be able to face myself. A disaster. I scoured apartment listings. I looked for white walls. A clean bathtub. I talked it over with Guillaume. We cried in each other's arms. It was the first time we'd touched in weeks. I couldn't believe we'd reached this point.

The book was going to be about an open marriage, but it was turning into something else. It ended up being about I don't know quite what anymore. About the torment of no longer loving someone who'd saved me, who could make me happy, who loved me, whom I loved. About no longer loving that person and loving someone else, someone imperfect, a stranger. No longer loving the man I wanted to love forever. Or dare I write it: no longer loving the man I had wanted to love forever.

::

Guillaume in Paris, 2012. He'd left at the beginning of October. The first, I think. He'd walked me to the bus stop. I had to work, hadn't managed to get the day off. I looked at him standing at the corner, knowing the days ahead would be hard. I came home that night to an empty apartment.

A few days earlier I'd written: "In six days, you'll be on a plane. I'll close the door behind you, set up a space to write and finally try to finish my novel. I'll tie my hands to the keyboard, chain my body to the chair. I'll only get up to attend to basic functions. I'll hope to reach a state of vertigo, total isolation, and I'll be able to let the idea flow free. I will live and breathe the book." I'd written those lines in the future, likely already knowing that things wouldn't go that way. I did write a lot those months we were apart, but mostly I'd wandered, written about longing, neglected my novel.

"If it weren't for the cat, I'd have already gone to my mother's. Even though the cat wakes me up at night with her extra claw clacking on the floor, her obsession with nudging things off my desk. I'm surprised at myself for being mean to her. I love that little cat. She looks after me. You're one of the few who know I can't sleep with the lights off, can't close the bedroom door. Without you here, the room seems to go on forever. It's a kind of inverse claustrophobia, where the space keeps expanding and I get lost."

I'd gotten through the months without him, my friends there to hold me up.

::

He showed up at the house around twenty to six. He rang the bell. I buzzed him in. He came upstairs, probably in the elevator, and knocked. I opened the door. I looked at him. I sat on the bench to give him time to take off his shoes. He said: I won't stay long.

We went into the office. I offered him a beer. He said no. He got up to go to the bathroom. I finished writing an email while he was gone. He came back, petted the cat. She liked him, had

59

never bitten him. I took it as a sign. I trusted her instincts, could rely on them. He came over and sat next to me, and while he looked for music on the computer I unbuckled his belt, unzipped his pants.

I put my shirt back on and cuddled in close to him. I said: you let me get close to you because you weren't afraid I'd get attached, because I'm married. But now, if I leave my husband, are you going to pull away? I'm afraid of not seeing you anymore. I'm being as honest as I can be. I know you don't want a relationship. We could keep seeing each other according to the rules, once a week.

I've forgotten the rest of the conversation. It's a flaw of mine, throwing out questions without listening to the answers. The answers must have been vague. Ambiguous. Hesitation, then an "I don't know." We kissed in the hall. He said: you're good for me.

I said: you're good for me too.

He left, and I slept alone that night.

::

The further I got in the novel, the more urgent it became for me to make a radical change in my life. For the moment, I didn't see that change coming. I didn't want the book to be a blip in my emotional development. A writerly experiment with misery. I had to be fully and truly committed. If I wanted to put writing at the centre of my existence, I had to go all the way. Solitude was the only possible answer. The act that would ask the most of me. I thought about what Annie Ernaux says in *L'écriture comme un couteau*: "I also resisted diving into the writing of *The Frozen Woman*. I suspected that, consciously or not, I was endangering my personal life, that when I finished the book I would be separated from my husband. Which is what happened."

Thinking so hard about the relationships in my life could only lead me to cast doubt on everything, on my marriage, myself. I was slipping. I wanted to slip.

::

I was alone in the canal, hair down to my feet and full of shells and dead leaves, seaweed under my arms. My breasts bare. I was singing *Wicked Game* à la Pipilotti Rist. But there was no one to hear me. Ten past ten, no moon. I was waiting for him, reviewing everything I had to say to him, most of it trivial. Would he come? Did he want me? An emotionally dependent mermaid. Only able to find happiness in another. I polished myself, scrubbed my skin until it glistened. I wanted to become that precious thing he'd want to keep forever.

::

My mother had been asking about my writing. I was vague, not wanting to tell her too much about the novel. I knew I'd eventually have no choice. I would have to prepare her, ask her not to read it or not to tell me if she did. I was too fond of avoidance. It was my preferred tactic in daily conflicts. Running away often seemed the best option. I dreaded my mother reading it. I dreaded my mother-in-law reading it even more. I'd always had the support of my family. I was lucky. They'd read all my books, passed my poems back and forth, hiding them under pillows like they were love poems. It would be difficult to keep them from reading this novel. Knowing this, I worked hard to not censor myself. One of my university professors used to talk about the books you could only write once your parents were dead. I didn't want to prove him right. I also couldn't wait that long. That feeling of time slipping through my fingers.

What would I have to write about in forty years? I say forty years, realizing there are not forty left. That it's unlikely my parents will live that long. I don't want them to die, would take their place a thousand times over. My fascination with death again. My anxiety over not being ready to die. So many people say they want to die in their sleep. I'm not one of them. I want to know when it's coming. I want to feel it, to be aware. Hence my fascination with suicide. A death that's deeper than death, one that's chosen, planned.

Guillaume told me he didn't want to have to talk about the book with his parents. He was afraid the blame would come back on him for the failings in our story, that he'd have to justify himself. We think that a man cheats because of sexual compulsions, and a woman because of unmet needs. We think: you couldn't keep your woman at home.

Despite our personalities, how we were careful not to conform, we found ourselves vacillating between the dominant ideal of the couple and our personal aspirations. Not even we could escape it.

::

I'd gone to write in a café, then met up with him when the bookstore closed. We'd walked with a coworker as far as the metro, then headed north. The coworker had his bike. We got to the apartment around eleven. We almost stopped for a beer, but I'd drunk too much that week already. We talked. He was tired. We lay down on the bed. I went down on him. We slept.

The next day I woke up before him. I got dressed. I stood at the foot of the bed and looked at him, still sleeping. I left the room, then the apartment. A step in the right direction. Untangling myself from passion's grip. By the time I reached the Beaubien metro I was free again. That's what I'd wanted to write. In reality, I'd looked at him from the foot of the bed. I'd crawled back in next to him. He woke up, pulled me close, noticed the dress, mumbled something. I told him I wanted to leave. We talked about it. I knew it was too late. I wouldn't be able to tear myself away again. We made love, held by each other's gaze, like in that Jacques Brel song.

::

It was my fault that my husband and I had stopped having sex. I don't really know why I'm using the word fault, maybe because I feel guilty about the drifting apart. It had been insidious. Longer interludes, fewer touches, fewer kisses. Until it became strange.

Talking to a friend in a bar, I realized the bizarre nature of the situation. I was married to one man and faithful to another.

The open relationship had allowed me to become whole. I was finding myself. I wanted a solitude I'd never wanted before. Between two men there was space for me to be alone.

I wondered about the future of my marriage. I didn't want to fall into the old trap of monogamy, to start it all again somewhere else. To bring one story to an end just to start another. I wanted to get divorced to be my own complete person, which I'd never really been in my adult life.

::

I'd arrived at his place at eight thirty. I sat on his bed while he finished tuning his guitar. He played a little bit. We went and sat on the balcony. He'd bought wine. It was nice. The spring, the warm May day, him. I listened to him talk. He sounded like an actor. He often spoke about his family. About his sister he said: I'm going to tell you something, but if you meet her you have to forget it.

I noted the possibility that she and I might meet some day. We went inside, had one more glass of wine.

He looped the rope around my neck. Then, all the rest. He got a little irritated with my questions about his orgasms. I wanted him to come at the same time as me, which almost never happened. I was obsessed with simultaneous orgasms in a way I'd thought normal until now. Apparently, that wasn't the shared goal of every sexual encounter. We stopped talking and went back to having sex. Afterward, we watched a few scenes from a couple of Antonioni movies. He showed me his favourite parts. I liked the way he analyzed things. Then we put on a horror movie. When I got scared, he held me tight in his arms until it was over.

I woke up before him. I liked watching him sleep, his chest rising and falling. I wondered if I loved him. Why was it so difficult to know?

That morning, we didn't have sex. We sat outside at a café drinking coffee instead.

: :

I wrote to him: if I get divorced, do you think we'll be together one day?

I needed to know because I wanted to see how I'd react. I needed to know if I could be in a relationship that couldn't ever evolve, in terms of time or commitment.

There was never a clear answer.

Finally he wrote: I don't know. That's a big question.

I wasn't totally satisfied but I understood. I would have said the same. I would've wanted to keep my options open. I would have left the door ajar, making sure it couldn't swing open on its own. You have to protect yourself from love.

::

I was supposed to meet a friend downtown. I was going to stay at her place while she was away at a residency. I was going to pick up the keys, pay her two weeks' rent.

::

We'd gone to a bar with people from work. We were celebrating someone's last day at the bookstore. We'd had a lot to drink, eaten pot brownies, partied late into the night. We took a taxi back to his place. That's probably where he lost his phone. We tried to find it using an app, without success. I took out my contact lenses, stuck them on his nipples. We laughed. Then we fell asleep.

I woke up before him. His phone disappearing had made me anxious. I was obsessed with recovering lost objects. When I was little, my favourite saint was Anthony of Padua. I got up. I kissed him. He said: why are you leaving so early?

I said: I want to let you sleep.

I walked. It was windy. I was listening to *OK Computer*. I still felt high. I'd forgotten my glasses at home so I could barely see. I was thinking about his phone. I walked for maybe an hour. To the restaurant where we'd eaten before going home. I asked the server if she'd found a phone. She pulled out a ring of keys, opened a drawer beneath the cash. Nothing. I went as far as Mont-Royal metro. I ran into friends there, a former couple. He had a broken arm. She looked beautiful. I told them I was looking for a phone. I must have seemed confused. I took the metro back to Beaubien. I bought five croissants, bananas, cherries. I went back to his place. I rang the bell three times. No answer. I went around to the back balcony and knocked. Still no answer. I sat down for a couple minutes.

I looked at my phone. I didn't want to leave. I'd come all this way for nothing. I felt ridiculous. A cliché of a woman who was totally infatuated, obsessed with a man. I went back over the events of the night before. We'd told a few work friends that we were seeing each other. Some had laughed. One had been angry.

Later in the night, we'd leaned in to kiss each other and that same guy knocked our heads together. Hard. I'd thought my nose was bleeding.

It started raining. A light rain. I got up and knocked again. Then, it started raining harder. So hard I thought it might start to hail. He appeared in the window. He opened the door. He didn't understand what I was doing there. I thought he must have heard me the first time, that he just didn't want to see me. But that the thought of the rain had softened him. He said: no, I was sleeping. The rain woke me up. I came to make sure the window was closed.

I told myself it would be better if I believed him. I said: can I come in? Can I lie down for a while?

I was soaked. I got undressed and collapsed on the bed. He lay down next to me. We tried to sleep for about twenty minutes. He said: we're obviously not going to sleep.

He kissed me. I climbed on top of him. He touched my face. His skin was hot. He put on a condom. I was still on top. I said: I love you, Seb.

He said: I love you too.

We had breakfast together. He made coffee. I ate cherries, watched his heart beating between his ribs.

∷

A little one bedroom in a quiet neighbourhood. Perfect for being alone. For writing. The walls were white, hung with a few photos, a few poems. I left the screen between the living room and bedroom open. There was a balcony. A kitchen at the back. A few utensils, a bowl, two cups, two pots. No toaster. No microwave. Just an oven and a coffee maker. The floors were wood. And just like at my parents' place, the gaps between the boards held hidden dangers. On my second morning there, a piece of glass got lodged in my foot. I had a phobia of glass shards. A very clear memory of my father, his thick fingers on my foot, blood, the sound of tweezers grasping at the glass and slipping off it again. This time, I managed to get it out without too much trouble. I placed the little shard on the windowsill to look at it.

He came to meet me after work. I knew he wouldn't be able to sleep there. The walls were too thin. He'd be afraid of making noise, or being woken by the neighbours. He sat down, kept his leather jacket on. We talked a little. He wanted to know why I'd seemed sad at work earlier. I'd gotten a message from Guillaume that said: just so we're clear, you've been cheating on me for a while now. Ever since I've been uncomfortable with what's going on. Things have been continuing according to your own set of rules and it really sucks.

I'd been in a meeting and just glanced at my phone. When I had the chance to answer, I wrote: I'll call you in a bit. Are we good?

To which he'd replied: let's not rehash the same conversation we've had twenty times. All it does is reassure me for a while and then you keep doing exactly what you're doing. Don't get me wrong, I was happy to see you yesterday, but clearly your attitude hasn't changed and it's just depressing.

I didn't know what to say. I understood his anger. I understood his pain. I just didn't know. The meeting ended. I stayed in the office. I cried. The time at my friend's place would give me space to think.

He came in. There were tissues near my computer and he asked if I'd been crying. I said no. Then we left for his place. It wasn't far. Maybe a fifteen-minute walk. Nothing had changed since the last time. We went to bed. We had sex. Slept.

The next day, we sat outside at a café and had breakfast. Two people who used to work at the bookstore walked by. They called out to us, laughing. I was so surprised to see them, I didn't know what to say. They kept going, walking toward the park.

We went into a bookstore. I looked for books by Claire Legendre, Christian Mistral, some collections of poetry. I thought about buying one by Renaud Longchamps, but didn't get anything in the end. He bought Moravia's *The Conformist*. He loved the Bertolucci film.

We went by his place. He wanted to lend me his toaster. I took it to make him happy. I almost never ate breakfast even though it was my favourite meal. I walked to the apartment. I sat on the balcony. I called Guillaume on Skype. I'd been having problems with the internet, and the connection was bad. It was nice to talk to him. We discussed his thesis. Then I started working. I wrote till seven. I took a shower. I watched

Polanski's *The Tenant*. Then I went out, with a pack of cigarettes and my headphones.

::

It was a forty-minute walk to the apartment from work. I went part of the way with a new employee. We talked about poetry, nothing new. I left him at the metro. He'd hesitated, unsure about kissing me goodbye on both cheeks. We parted on an awkward note. I took out my phone to call Guillaume. We talked about my novel. Edits I had to make, my doubts and my certainties. He was a good listener, asked the right questions. I'd reread the whole thing that day. I had a lot to think about. Then we talked about dinner on Wednesday. Friends from Quebec City were coming to town. We would have to see them. I told Guillaume I'd go back to Rosemont to sleep after the dinner. He was annoyed. He found it humiliating. I didn't know what to tell him. I understood how he felt, but I didn't feel I could stay. I thought maybe it was better if I didn't go. I'd just skip the whole thing, not see them at all. It was hard to know how to react to his emotions. On one hand, he was able to express his feelings; on the other, it seemed that all he wanted to do was to distance himself, to push me away. That any attempt I made would end in failure. I didn't love him the right way. But it was like he had nothing left for me. He was busy with his thesis day and night. I gave him free rein, and the apartment. So he could work, so he could focus.

: :

There was a round mark beneath my breasts. An imprint of teeth. I took a photo of it with my phone.

: :

I'd bought a bottle of white wine. I arrived around seven. Mathieu was already there. Christo too. Guillaume poured me a glass of rosé. I took advantage of a heated debate about hunting to motion Guillaume over to our bedroom. We kissed. I felt good. I jerked him off. He came. We kissed again. We'd been gone for maybe eight minutes. Nobody seemed to have noticed. I finished the wine. We opened a bottle of white. The others arrived a little later. We ate. We drank the seven bottles. There was just liquor left. I took out some pot brownies and we ate them. We smoked a bit. Guillaume passed around a bottle of vodka. We started dancing. Then we all ended up in dresses.

My dresses. We lay on the bed, all seven of us. We were happy.

It was getting late. I took a taxi with Anne-Marie. She got out at Saint-Laurent and Beaubien. I continued on to De Lorimier. I texted him. He was waiting for me on the sidewalk, in his slippers. I threw my arms around him. We went inside. I tried to be quiet. We went to bed. I showed him videos of my friends. I was laughing. He didn't really react. We had sex. I was too nauseous to go down on him. We fell asleep.

We woke up around ten. Had sex again. I couldn't come, but he did, on my stomach.

We went out for breakfast. The conversation was heavy. He thought I was accusing him of something. I probably was. We'd been sleeping together for over six months. We had two options: stop or keep going. We didn't have to decide right then, but I knew it was starting to wear on Guillaume, and I didn't want it to be him who brought things to an end. I wanted us to be able to talk about it first.

We walked to his place. I said: can I kiss you on the stairs?

He smiled, said: yes.

He opened the door. We kissed. He slid his hand up my skirt. I kissed him harder. He asked me in. We went to his room. We had sex. I came, on top of him. I had to leave, he had to go to work.

: :

Seeing my friends, the same friends who'd been at our wedding, who had been with us through the tough times, gave me hope in my marriage again. Did love only last three years or could I look forward to something beyond being comfortably bored? I'd made a promise in front of the people I cared for most that I would work for this relationship. I owed it to them to at least try a little. But I also had a strong feeling that this new connection was important. That I'd never find another soul as close to my own. It was a battle between passion and reason.

The dinner had plunged me back into my life for a moment. I loved my friends, my husband, my cat, my apartment. On paper, everything was as it should be. A perfect life. So why didn't I want to live it anymore?

: :

I had no voice. I wanted to return to my canals. To my routines. To comfort. I wanted to finish the book and move on. I tried not to be influenced by thoughts of how people would react to the novel. Especially Guillaume and Sébastien. They would both be disappointed. I knew that much. Sébastien would think I hadn't managed to convey the intensity of our nights together. Guillaume would learn my secrets, think me even more underhanded. Both would feel like they'd been played. They'd be right. I'd been played too. I was destroying my life for this book. As I write this, I really believe it. I am alone in a white apartment. The couch is covered in tissues. There's a gift bag on a chair that's been there since last week, for a birthday I skipped so I could write instead. Perrier bottles everywhere. Dirty dishes. Anxiety. Pages of my manuscript on the wall, edited and annotated. A fly that's been buzzing around the living room for hours. Me, in the middle of the room. Half naked. Panicking. Unable to choose. A choice has to be made. A choice always has to be made. Hidden behind the text. Everything for the text. The camera always recording. A video of me eating. A video of me reading. A video of me writing. A video of me watching the video. The height of narcissism. To make a novel of yourself. To make yourself into a novel to give yourself a little meaning. Mostly, to be afraid of not existing. The mermaid exists. The mermaid is writing a novel and filming herself as she writes. She takes a photo of herself. For her archives. The mermaid is writing a novel because she has no voice.

::

I couldn't take being shut in the apartment any longer. I got dressed. Put on my headphones. *Third* by Portishead. I went out. Walked down Papineau to Laurier. Then west. I stopped to buy a coffee. I wanted to work all night. The bookstore was closing. I sat down outside until a coworker waved me in. I chatted with him. Sébastien was counting the cash. We left, walked to Rosemont metro. Then to my place. He came in. The living room was a mess. I was embarrassed. I went to get him a glass of water. I knew he'd start reading the pages on the wall. He read a lot of them. I was afraid of what he was going to say. He smiled, a little uncomfortable. He said: I sound like a jerk.

I said: no you don't.

He said: I sound like the boyfriend in that Nelly Arcan book, *Hysteric*. I hated that guy.

I smiled.

I told him I would be sad to lose him. That I didn't think I was the one who'd get him to commit. He said: if you can't, who will?

He wrapped his arms around me. Two tears spilled out. He wiped them away. He said he didn't want to lose me. I cried some more. I think he cried too.

::

She arrived twenty minutes after calling me. We made coffee. She didn't know about the open marriage. Well, she knew a bit. A friend had mentioned something. We talked about it. She listened. It felt good to talk. She said: what's his name?

I said: Sébastien.

She'd brought me a dress. I put it on. I took down my hair. She wet it in the bathroom sink. I took off the dress. We moved the table. I stood near the wall. Water ran down my chest. She took some pictures. She didn't seem satisfied. I couldn't concentrate. I was too anxious. We put everything back. I got dressed again. We finished our coffee.

I was the queen of nothing in this story. I was stuck. Painted into a corner. Caught in a trap.

Alone. Totally alone. It was raining. I looked at my credit card balance. I wanted to take a taxi down to the port. I wanted to go home. But I didn't want to go home. I didn't want to give in. He always saved me in the end, my giant. My Adjutor.

I went out. I walked to the overpass at Papineau and De Carrières. I looked down at the traffic, listening to Antony and the Johnsons. I felt better. I went back to my manuscript.

::

He came over after work. Stopped in for a minute on his way home. He started reading the pages on the wall again. He said: it sounds like I do all this to you and you don't want it. Like I'm subjecting you to it. You sound a bit like a victim.

That made me angry. I got up and read the paragraph. I said: I ask you to do it. I say that I want you to keep doing it, forever. It's written right there.

I wasn't a victim. I never had been. Even when I could've been. Not even when that guy forced himself on me. When he kept going until I told him his nose was bleeding. I hadn't been a victim. I'd written a poem, published it in my book. A year later I was invited to read at a poetry event. I saw that he'd be there. I chose the reading knowing that. And he was there. I brought him up on stage. I made him read the poem in front of everyone. From the outside, the performance seemed to fall flat. From the inside, it was perfect. I knew. He knew. A little act of revenge.

Why now, sleeping with someone I loved, did I seem like a victim?

::

People read me as vulnerable. I take care to look pretty. Perfectly groomed. Perfectly made up. Batting my lashes with timed grace. Resting my elegant hands with poise. My fragility is my strength. But what they don't know is that I'm a force of destruction, an enchantress. The prey and the predator. Both at once. I'm the one who does the asking. I'm the one who sets the limit.

::

I went back to the apartment in the port. I unpacked my suitcases. Slept in the office.

A message from Marie-Claude said she wouldn't be back in Montreal for another week. She wanted to know if I would stay longer at her place. I said I'd think about it, that I'd already left, but that I could go back.

::

I went home after breakfast with Sébastien.
I told Guillaume I'd slept there. He'd thought
I was at Marie-Claude's. He was angry. We had
a long conversation. The same one as always.
He was right. I was breaking the rules. I was
cheating on him.

I ate a bowl of pasta in front of my computer. He
was working on his thesis in the next room. He
slept in the office that night.

::

I'd started lying in the book. Strangely, I was
lying less in real life.

::

My tarot cards said I was incapable of making
a decision. The *Two of Swords*. A woman sitting
before an expanse of water. A few rocks rise
above its surface. She holds two blades crossed
in front of her face. She is blindfolded. She is
stuck.

My cards were right. I couldn't choose.

::

We sat side by side in the booth. The server had taken the time to place two orange slices in our glasses of beer. Things were tense. I wanted him to tell me we'd never be together. He said nothing. *Love Hurts* came on. We cracked up. We couldn't help it. The song ended. We sat there silent, watching some guys play pool. I'd finished my beer. I really wanted him. I said: fuck me hard. I said it twice. He wanted me too. We said we'd go to a hotel, the same one as a few months before. We went outside. It was raining. I didn't have a condom. He didn't either. I knew I was ovulating. I decided to go home. It was difficult.

::

I was in Baie-Sainte-Catherine with friends. We'd rented a cottage. Or more of a rustic cabin. Fourteen bunks, two mini-fridges, a toaster, a coffee maker. We ate outside. We charred our vegetables black in the fire. We laughed, called it our hot-cuisine. Guillaume was in Bordeaux for a few weeks. It was nice to get away. We were deep in our New Age nature escape. We built a makeshift sauna, swam naked in the river. A mud bath, a baptism, a new beginning.

One morning over coffee, I told two of my friends about the novel. I was questioning the

concept of privacy, the ethics of exposing intimate details. I was wondering if it was a betrayal.
My friends thought I shouldn't edit out too
much. There was nothing that was too difficult
to cut, but cutting anything would affect the
story.

Guillaume had said he'd prefer not to read
the book. It made me feel a bit like I'd be hiding
something from him. I would've rather that he
be curious, that he want to read it and that he
challenge me on what I wrote. I knew he'd be
very critical, that he wouldn't spare my ego,
wouldn't let me off the hook. It was too easy to
write a book with a single point of view, to erase,
even unconsciously, the troubling details and the
shameful parts. The abuse, the malevolence, the
malice, the pain, the betrayal, the disgust. It was
too easy. I'd betrayed him. I'd promised before
family and friends to at least try. I could agree
to rewriting in that context, because it would be
about getting closer to the truth.

The conversation did me good.

::

My time away had made it hard to go back to
the bookstore. I wanted to put my personal life
back in order, devote some time to my family, my

friends, myself. I'd left Baie-Sainte-Catherine determined to quit. I wrote the letter on Monday. Tuesday, my boss was away, so I sent him a text: hi, sorry to do this over text, but I wanted to let you know as soon as possible (especially with your vacation coming up). I'm giving my notice. Should I send a letter to HR so they can start looking right away?

He replied: yes. Thanks. I'll call you shortly.

I was talking with some coworkers when he called. I was nervous. He asked why I was leaving. I said it was my waning motivation, my writing projects. I could tell he wasn't satisfied. It's true that I had tried to quit that spring and he'd talked me out of it. He'd said: you know, not all dreams come true.

I'd given in and stayed on even though I barely did anything at work anymore, spent my shifts chatting. So I was apprehensive. He wanted firm, real plans. I told him that Guillaume was leaving for Switzerland, that I was going with him. And it worked. He was encouraging. In the moment, I didn't feel like I was lying. There was still a slim chance that I would go with Guillaume to Basel.

Soon everyone was talking about my trip to Switzerland. Another imaginary trip.

::

He came to pick me up at the Laval station. He had his mother's car. He showed me a few streets in Saint-Jérôme. We stopped for a beer, then went on to his parents' place. A residential neighbourhood, a typical suburb: a park on the corner, garages, hedges, silence after eleven. He took me through the house. The décor was somber, with few details to reveal anything about the people who lived there. A few drawings by his niece on the walls in the basement were the only sign of life. We looked at the photos of him as a child in his father's room. We would be sleeping there.

It was late. We went to bed. We started kissing. I started hyperventilating while I was going down on him. I panicked. I think I lost consciousness for a few moments. When I came to, it was several minutes before I could speak. I couldn't get the words out.

I managed to say goodnight as he switched off the lamp.

The next morning I had a headache. He made me oatmeal. We ate, read in the garden. A cat was wandering around the yard. We petted it, gave it some food. His sister came to pick us up.

I barely spoke in the car. We took the train to Montreal.

I think he said something about having been really frightened when I'd started hyperventilating. I searched online to try to understand what was happening to me. Lots of talk of *la petite mort* but always related to orgasm. I didn't think I was having an orgasm at that moment. I knew I'd obscured some facts about those attacks in my writing. It had happened a few times with Guillaume. Never with anyone else. Since I'd been seeing Sébastien, it was more intense, more frightening. I knew I was eliding details to avoid steering the novel to places I didn't want to go.

::

I was in the bathroom when she called. I called her back. She'd been off work for just a few hours. She'd be in Dawson for four days before going back to camp. I blurted out that I wanted to come see her in Yukon. I asked if there was space for me in her trailer. I could pay her boss for expenses, for food at least. I'd do the cleaning, wash the dishes. I also told her to mention it to her boyfriend, because I didn't want to create any conflict. But I wasn't the type of ex who'd suddenly show up uninvited anyway. She seemed excited by the idea. I wanted to be alone. I pictured myself crossing Canada by bus with my headphones, my computer, a few books. I would curl up with my knees on the seat in front of me and sleep for hours. I knew Yukon would do me good. Or maybe I'd go to Europe. Maybe Prague. Prague, by myself. To finish the book. Prague or Brussels.

::

Lies are a device often used in fiction.

::

We were by the canal. He'd come back from Bordeaux the day before. We'd been having a day of ups and downs. Full of difficult discussions on the future of our marriage, what the end would entail, the possibility of therapy, my problems, his, ours. Our commitments, what we wanted our marriage to be. We were calm. We needed to make a decision but we couldn't get anywhere. I still imagined us growing old together. There was a loss to be grieved.

We were close to the Five Roses sign. I was trying to explain my desire to be alone, the challenge that it represented.

I realized I hadn't written in days. I'd broken the rules of the novel. The fiction I'd imposed on myself to write the book was swallowing me whole. I'd stopped writing it and started living it.

::

It was late. Guillaume was jet-lagged, already asleep. I received a screenshot of a flight reservation: Montreal–Barcelona, Brussels–Montreal. Nine hundred and seventy dollars, the beginning of September. Sébastien had bought his tickets. I had to make a decision.

I went to bed.

Guillaume woke me up. He said: I put the coffee on the stove, can you keep an eye on it while I go to the grocery store?

I got up. The coffee whistled. I turned off the stove. I took a shower, got dressed. Guillaume still wasn't back. I started making my breakfast. He came in and dropped a bunch of bananas on the table, turned on some music. Two slices of toast for him and two for me. I thought about squeezing a grapefruit. I started buttering my toast. His were slathered in vegan butter, peanut butter, topped with banana slices and sesame seeds. I mentioned the trip to Europe with Sébastien. He didn't say anything. I was surprised. I didn't understand. I thought we'd talk about it. Then he said he wasn't hungry anymore. He got up, grabbed his bag and left the apartment. I went into my office and cried.

I walked down Avenue du Parc toward the port and thought about the dream I'd had, back in November already. The one where I was going to the airport with Sébastien and we kissed. All this had started with a dream of a trip I didn't even go on. I just waved and watched him leave.

I went home. The two slices of toast were still on the table. I started crying again.

::

Guillaume hadn't come home. He'd gone to a cottage with friends. He texted: we'll talk tomorrow.

I called my ex. I'd been thinking of her a lot. I thought of the courage it had taken her to leave me five years earlier. We talked.

I slept.

It was already the next day. I didn't have to work. I spent the day waiting. He came home. For some reason I smiled when he walked in.

His toast was still on the table. The bananas had turned black. A few fruit flies hovered over the plate. In my first novel, there's a passage about a tomato left in the refrigerator by an ex-girlfriend, and the main character can't bring herself to throw it out.

A long two hours of talking. Back and forth on the subject of separation. Turning the situation around, dividing the furniture, maybe getting back together. He would obviously keep the apartment. I'd have to go elsewhere. There was also his brother's wedding the next week.

And then I don't really know how but we weren't in the middle of separating anymore. We'd put it off for now.

I'd planned to sleep at Sébastien's. Guillaume knew. I got there late. I'd bought beer. I drank one, smoked a cigarette. I talked the whole time then we went into the bedroom. We tried to have sex, but it didn't work. We laughed a lot at least.

∷

I bought a plane ticket. Montreal–Prague, Brussels–Montreal. I'd finish the novel in the Czech Republic then I'd go to Berlin and end my trip in Brussels. I would be alone because I needed to be alone. Then I'd probably run out of money. I'd come back to Montreal. And after that, I didn't know.

For the moment, I was at my friend Charles' place. Taking care of his plants and his cat. I spent entire days on the living-room couch. I didn't move, got up only to go to the bathroom or rummage in the fridge. Books and clothes were strewn all around me. Empty Perrier and iced-tea bottles, empty packs of cigarettes, scribbled pages, pencils, a pillow, a sheet. There was only the cat to draw me out of my thoughts. A few times an hour he came and nipped at my arm so I would cuddle or feed him.

I'd lost all motivation for the novel. I was coming to the end of it feeling weak and small. I was a coward. I'd broken my contract. I wouldn't see the story through to the end. I was realizing that I'd tried to use other people for my fiction. I was realizing that no one but me wanted to be a character in this story. No one but me found it fulfilling. No one but me needed it to give life meaning.

I'd tumbled from fiction into reality. I found myself with a complicated mess on my hands, the bed I'd made for myself. I only wanted to lie if it served a narrative thread. I didn't see the point otherwise. I felt I'd lost my grip on the project, my thoughts had fragmented. My mistake had been to forget all this was fiction. I'd forced feelings, turns of events, and it had worked against me.

So I was avoiding writing. I was going in circles. I was obsessing.

::

I sent the manuscript to my publisher. I'm sick of writing in the past tense. This is no longer fiction. I'm in a car on my way to Montreal. I'm filming myself again. The camera captures a tired version of myself. I'm so stressed that I haven't slept. Last night I dreamed my poetry publisher was dropping me. I got up to write. I went back to bed an hour later. I'm anxious, waiting to see what Éric says about the book. Maybe he won't like it. If he doesn't, I'm not sure how I'll feel. Energy wasted. I leave for Prague in eight days. There's a few places I can stay. Sébastien leaves for Europe six days after I do. He'll go to Spain and then Belgium. I think he'd like us to meet up. But I'm not really sure what I want. I'm afraid this will keep going, that it will never end.

::

When I film myself writing, I create a moment. I get ready, I put on makeup, I find the perfect angle. It becomes my own little performance, a personal mise en scène. I'd rather live in virtual reality. I don't want real life. I don't want a body. I prefer fiction. Guillaume told me: you have trouble distinguishing between reality and fiction.

And I think he's right. I exist in the reflection of my camera lens. People who suffer from depersonalization or derealization feel detached from their own mental processes, a feeling like sleepwalking, a foreignization of the self. They have an obsessive tendency to observe themselves, a need to validate their presence in the world. This novel responds to the same mechanism. Writing it anchors me in the world, lets me feel alive, lets me move, lets me work. Without the book, I am an empty shell.

::

Who exactly was I lying to?

::

I'd been at Charles' place for a few days. I needed to buy a book for a friend. I walked through

94

Little Italy, then Mile End. I dropped into Drawn & Quarterly, scanned the poetry shelf. There were a lot of English books I wanted to read. But the store was closing. I left empty-handed. I walked to Renaud-Bray. I quickly found the book I wanted and grabbed a blue highlighter. Sébastien rang it up, gave me a discount. I stayed until close. We walked. His friends were in a bar that was on our way. We stopped in to say hi. That girl who doesn't like me was there. She wouldn't look at me. I felt uneasy. We left. At Charles' place we took Oxycodone. We felt so calm. I drove him home. The night ended in a fight. I needed clarification again. There were still no answers. He said nothing.

We were nothing and we had no future. I went home, slept terribly.

The next day I had trouble finding the car in the streets of Villeray. For a moment I thought I'd lost it.

::

I was leaving for Prague the next day. I was extremely stressed. I still hadn't heard from my publisher. And I didn't know where I would sleep Tuesday night. Things were weird with Guillaume. I knew he wanted us to have sex.

I couldn't even imagine it. I had almost no sex drive at that point. I was afraid of freaking out, of hyperventilating. I couldn't control it anymore.

I was sitting in a Montreal café. Devouring a vegan Caesar salad like some kind of animal. I could see it in my webcam. Portishead played in the background.

::

I'd been in Prague for two days. I was staying with friends of friends in an apartment in Vinohrady. I walked a lot. Every night I dreamed that my poetry publisher accepted my manuscript, or rejected it. I woke up exhausted. I was still waiting, and waiting for news about the novel too.

::

I went to Kafka's grave, for something to do. I'd never read him. I didn't like the idea of visiting someone's grave. I realized that I didn't like anything. I walked through the city. I didn't like anything. I only liked sitting in front of my computer. And I liked the idea of writing a book. The idea of my life being printed/kept/archived/photographed.

I still wasn't sure what I'd hoped to find here. A planetary alignment. A bit of magic. An ending for a book.

Prague. Confirmation of the novel. Going all in. Proof of my commitment. But why prove it this way, by coming to this idealized elsewhere?

::

I am withholding information. There are things I am not saying. What I choose to hide is what I most need to say. I know exactly what it is. I don't want to write it down. But I also know it's part of the story. I write around it, resist it. I probably won't find the courage to get there. Not now. Not in this book.

::

I was in a new apartment. Further from the city centre, in a communist building under renovation. There was dust everywhere. My room could barely fit a cot and my suitcase. To open the window, I had to close the door. To open the door, I had to close the window. No hot water. Ants everywhere. I drank tea, ate Saturn peaches and oatmeal. Slept badly.

From the beginning, I knew I'd go meet Sébastien. I was hiding it. Keeping it out of the novel. We'd meet on the fifteenth of September. For now, I was alone in Prague. It was the fourth, almost the fifth. I was dreaming of buying a ticket back to Montreal. To get myself out of this relationship. Again. I didn't understand why I'd chosen to lie to Guillaume.

::

I felt compelled to justify my literary approach, my decision to write autofiction in 2016, ten years after Nelly Arcan.

In one sense, it was automatic. That's what I preferred to read, what I related to. Not necessarily autofiction but deeply personal stories, ones that spilled off the page. No shaping, no representations. Creating characters didn't really appeal to me anymore. What would I do with those invented lives?

I talked to Guillaume over Skype. I told him I felt like I'd been split in two. Part of me living, part of me watching myself live. I wondered if I might have a dissociative identity disorder. Maybe caused by an earlier trauma. I tried to dig up memories I may have repressed. It's not easy to recover what has been repressed. I was a bit of a hypochondriac too, when it came to mental illness. A hypochondriac and paranoid. Attentive to detail, to the deterioration of my mind, my loss of control, my moments of absence. I felt like I was drifting outside of myself. I said: I'm getting weird. Which meant I was on the edge of a cliff. It happened sometimes. Especially when I was alone. It was hard not to see anyone, to stay cloistered in the apartment. I thought of Mathilde, a character in my first novel. The spiral. Confinement drives you mad. The novel was driving me mad.

::

He called on his way back from the beach. It was six thirty in the morning in Prague. Six thirty in the morning in Barcelona too. The sun was rising. I said I wanted to go back to Montreal. He didn't understand. We talked for a long time. Agreed to talk again the next day. I slept a little.

He called again that afternoon.

I wanted to stop seeing him. To save what we had from a slow death. No life, no death. A dream.

::

The Vltava is pretty in the afternoon. Vltava, from the old Germanic *wilt ahwa*, or wild water. I lie down by the water. The tourists don't see

99

me, busy looking at the statues on the bridge, immersed in their cameras or phones. I like being invisible. I'm never a woman in my dreams anymore. I'm a magical creature, a sea monster. I am disappointed. I sharpen my teeth into points. I'm done dreaming. I bite. I kill. A destructive power, a myth, a demon on the inside. Nothing left of the romantic heroine.

I let the sun wash over me. I watch the sky swirl.

::

Maybe my interest in intimate stories lies in the encounter with the other. Without falsehood or façade. A proximity otherwise impossible. Because for the novel to work, the author must tell the truth. A *huis clos* of the soul, no exit. A private interview. The closest you can get to entering someone else's world.

And, in the end, only literature could bring me a slight sense of wholeness. Only literature. And if I was in this tiny room in Letná that was crawling with ants, with no hot water, if I was cold, if I was crying, if I wasn't leaving Prague, it wasn't because of Sébastien. It was because I wanted to write a novel. From the beginning, I had wanted to write a novel.

QC FICTION

Current & Upcoming Books

Visit **qcfiction.com** for details and to subscribe
to a full season of QC Fiction titles.

Printed by Imprimerie Gauvin
Gatineau, Québec